VIKING KESTREL

Viking Penguin Inc., 40 West 23rd Street, New York, New York 10010, U.S.A.

Penguin Books Canada Limited, 2801 John Street, Markham, Ontario, Canada L3R 1B4

First published in Great Britain by Julia MacRae Books, a division of Franklin Watts Ltd., 1986

First American Edition

Published in 1987

Copyright © Valerie Littlewood, 1986

All rights reserved

Printed in Belgium ▨

1   2   3   4   5   90   89   88   87   86

Library of Congress catalog card number: 86-40195

ISBN 0-670-81433-4

The Season Clock

Valerie Littlewood

Viking Kestrel

In a hollow cavern, deep below the roots of an old oak tree, Father Time kept watch on the Season Clock, tending it with loving care. For it was here that Father Time saw to the changing of the Seasons, winding the Season Clock carefully so that Spring, Summer, Autumn, and Winter all came round at their proper time.

Father Time's young apprentice, Sam, helped him look after the Season Clock and studied all its movements. But he was never allowed to touch it.

One day, when Father Time was in the outside world with Autumn, Sam sat with Spring and Summer. He was bored.

"I'm tired of books and learning," he said. "I want an adventure."

"Why don't you wind the clock?" said Spring.

"Oh, I couldn't do *that*," said Sam.

"Why not?" asked Summer. "Are you afraid? Perhaps you are afraid of the Season Catcher?"

"Of course I'm not!" shouted Sam as he ran from the room.

But Sam should have been afraid, for at that very moment
the Season Catcher lurked outside in the Autumn
twilight. The Season Catcher was a miserable creature
who hated all light and sun, all gaiety and laughter.
He and his demons did their best to steal color and light from
everything they could find. They hated all the
Seasons.

Sam didn't give a thought to the Season Catcher, or to anything else for that matter. "I'm not afraid," he muttered to himself as he clambered into the works of the Season Clock. He swung the great lever backward and forward, backward and forward, until all the wheels and cogs spun faster and faster, faster and faster.

Suddenly the Clock was out of control.
Bells rang, springs sprang, wheels clanged. The noise was
terrible. Spring and Summer ran from the old oak tree
in panic. That was the chance the Season Catcher and his
demons had been waiting for. A host of demons
pushed Spring and Summer onto the Season Catcher's
horse and bore them away in triumph.

"Oh, what have I done?" cried Sam in terror, seeing
the confusion all around him.

Sam rushed outside.

"I must find Father Time," he said, and he ran shouting through the woods.

At last he found Father Time in a clearing with Autumn. He sobbed out his story.

"It's all my fault," he said. "I played with the Season Clock and now Spring and Summer have been taken by the Season Catcher. What shall we do?"

"Sam," said Father Time sternly, "you must stay here while I find the Season Catcher. You have done enough damage for one day." He set off with Autumn, leaving Sam behind.

I can't wait here, thought Sam. I must follow them. Maybe there will be *some* way I can help.

Keeping his distance, Sam followed Father Time. Soon he reached the dark and gloomy castle of the Season Catcher.

There on the steps sat Winter, his head in his hands.

"Father Time," he said sorrowfully, "I tried to follow Spring and Summer when the noise of the Clock woke me. But the Season Catcher was too fast for me and now he has them imprisoned inside his castle, locked away in the dungeon. I can do no more."

Sam slipped past as Winter was talking and crept to the dungeon window. Inside he saw Spring and Summer huddled together. But the walls were thick and the iron bars across the window were strong. It was impossible to get in.

"Spring! Summer!" Sam called through the window. "It's me, Sam. How can I help you?"

"The Season Catcher has the key," said Spring, "but you will never get to him. He lives right at the top of the castle and there are guards everywhere."

Carefully and quietly Sam climbed to the top of the castle. He slipped in through a window . . .

and down a corridor into a great banquet hall. The Season Catcher lay sprawled asleep across the remains of a huge feast. Slowly, Sam crept past the Season Catcher and gently slipped the key off the mantel.

Outside the castle, Autumn had spread a thick blanket of fog that seeped in through the castle windows and doors. "What is all this?" said the guards, wiping their eyes as the fog stole through the damp corridors of the castle. They did not see Sam dodging in and out of the fog. Soon he had reached the dungeon with the precious key.

"Come quickly," he said to Spring and Summer. Together they made their way outside to Father Time. They were safe!

Back at the old oak tree, Father Time put the Season Clock back into working order. "That's better," he said. "Now when Autumn comes inside, Winter will be ready to go outside and the Seasons will run as they should."

Then he looked at Sam. "I should be angry with you," he said. "You cannot meddle with the Seasons. But I will forgive you this time for you were brave in the end. Now let us get on with your lessons."

And that is just what they did.